SLEEPING BEAUTY

CHARLES PERRAULT

The sun was shining and the birds were singing, but the Queen was unhappy as she swam in her lake. "Oh, how I wish for a child," she sighed.

A frog who was perched on a nearby lily pad heard her wish. "By this time next year, you shall have a daughter!" he croaked. Then he dived into the weeds and was gone.

The frog's words came true. The next year, the King and Queen had a beautiful baby daughter. "The roses are just beginning to bloom," said the King. "Let's call her Rose, and give her the most magnificent christening ever known."

"What a lovely idea!" said the Queen. "We must invite everyone we know."

"And the thirteen fairies," added the King.

"My love," the Queen reminded him, "the law of the Kingdom says that fairies must eat from golden plates. And we only have twelve."

"Well, twelve fairies are enough then," decided the King.

On Rose's christening day, everyone in the palace celebrated. There was a grand feast, and the guests sang and danced until it was time for the fairies to present their gifts to the royal baby.

The first fairy gave her the gift of Beauty, the second gave her Grace. One by one, the other fairies gave Rose a Sweet Voice, Kindness, Health, Gentleness, Truth, Goodness, Friendship, Happiness, and a Sense of Humor. But, before the twelfth fairy could speak, the ballroom suddenly turned dark. The wind howled through an open window, an owl hooted, and everyone shivered.

Standing beside Rose's cradle was a small, bent figure dressed all in black. Her green eyes gleamed. It was the thirteenth fairy.

"You did not invite me," sneered the thirteenth fairy, "but here I am, and here is my gift. On her fifteenth birthday, the Princess will prick her finger on the spindle of a spinning wheel and she will die."

With these evil words, she vanished. The wind stopped howling and the owl was silent. In her cradle, the tiny Princess cried softly.

Then the twelfth fairy stepped forward and said quietly, "I can not undo that evil magic, but I can soften it. Rose *will* prick her finger, but she will not die. Instead, she and all within the palace will fall asleep — until one day a Prince's kiss will wake her."

Immediately the King ordered that every spinning wheel in the Kingdom be destroyed. Huge bonfires were lit in each village, and a thousand spinning wheels were burned.

The years flew by, and Rose grew up happily with the fairies' gifts. She was loved by all who knew her. On her fifteenth birthday, her parents gave her a splendid party.

Shortly before the palace clock struck six, Rose said, "Let's play hide and seek!" Her young guests hid in closets, under huge tables, and behind heavy curtains, while the seeker covered his eyes and began to count. Rose tiptoed up a winding staircase to a turret at the top of a tower where nobody had been for years.

It was very dark and musty in the turret. Rose was beginning to wish she had not hidden there when she saw a dusty door. She wrote her name in the dust, then pushed the door gently. It swung slowly open into a tiny room.

"Come in, my dear," whispered a strange voice.

Rose saw an old woman dressed in black, sitting beside a large wheel. The room grew darker, the wind blew outside and an owl hooted. Rose shivered.

"What's that funny thing?" Rose asked.

"Why, a spinning wheel, my dear." The old woman turned her pale, wrinkled face and watched Rose with gleaming green eyes. "I'm making cloth for a dress. Come closer . . . see how the spindle dances as the thread runs around it."

Rose had never seen a spinning wheel before and she was curious. She held out her hand to touch the bobbing spindle. "Ouch! It hurts!" she cried. At once she fell into a deep sleep.

The wind stopped, the owl grew silent, and warmth and light returned. The old woman had vanished.

The King and Queen stopped talking in the middle of a conversation and fell asleep. The young guests fell asleep in their hiding places, their fingers on lips that were about to say, "Shh!"

The clock stopped ticking, its hands frozen. Even the royal guard fell asleep.

In the kitchen, the cook's cat slept outside a mouse hole, while the frightened mouse slept inside. The cook fell asleep with her hand raised, ready to spank the naughty kitchen boy. The poor boy slept on her knee, while the glass goblet he had broken lay in pieces on the floor.

The palace dog, who always seemed to be dozing, slept even more soundly. The seeker slept standing up, his hands still covering his eyes. A fly hung in the air over a jam-covered spoon.

Up in the turret, the spiders were still and silent in their webs. The spinning wheel stopped spinning, and Rose remained in a deep sleep.

Days passed, and then weeks. Months turned into years and still more years. After ten years, a hedge of roses had grown all around the palace. After twenty, the palace was hidden completely. Ninety years passed, and the thicket of roses, weeds and thistles had grown into a forest.

The story of the Sleeping Beauty spread throughout the world. Many brave men tried to break through the forest to find her, but none could. One day, however, a handsome Prince arrived from a far-off land. Though cruelly scratched by the thorns and brambles, he hacked his way through the forest with his sword. It was tiring work, and his strength had almost given out when a very strange thing began to happen.

The cruel thorns softened, and roses began to bloom on the briars. He moved as if by magic through the branches. Soon he found himself at the palace gates.

A hundred years had passed since Rose's fifteenth birthday, but in the palace, time had stood still. The Prince opened the heavy palace doors. He passed among the sleeping party guests and climbed the same winding staircase the Princess had climbed a hundred years before.

At the top of the staircase he saw *Rose* written on the dusty door. And inside the turret room he found the sleeping girl. He had never seen anyone so beautiful. Slowly, as if in a dream, he bent his head and kissed her.

The Princess woke immediately. "I have waited so long for you," she said, gazing up at him.

At once everyone in the palace awoke. The King turned to the Queen and said, "I quite agree with you, my dear." The mouse scuttled further down the hole, away from the hissing cat. The dog rolled over. The naughty kitchen boy scrambled off the cook's lap and she slapped her own knee instead. The fly landed on the jam-covered spoon. And the palace clock finally struck six.

The seeker took his hands from his eyes and called out, "Ready!" The children in their hiding places giggled, fingers on their lips, and whispered, "Shh!"

Rose smiled up at her brave Prince. Many years later, when Rose and the Prince were married, they would often tell their children the strange tale of the thirteenth fairy, the spinning wheel, and the hundred sleeping years.

The first written version of the charming tale of the ***Sleeping Beauty*** is found in French writer Charles Perrault's collection, *Contes de ma mère l'oye* in 1697, translated into English as *Tales of Mother Goose* in 1729. Perrault was trained as a lawyer, but his poems and essays made him a leading literary figure; he was elected to the Académie Française in 1671. His theories on the nature of literature involved him in the famous "quarrel of the ancients and the moderns" (about the relative worth of ancient and modern literature).